Illustrations by
Oksana Basarab

"Fasten your seat belts ladies and gentlemen, we're soon going to land," said the stewardess.

"Look Samantha," said her mother, "you can see Kennedy Air Base out of the window."

Samantha couldn't wait to get there, she had won a competition to be the first young person to fly in a space shuttle, which was a rocket a little like a plane which could go into space and then fly back.

Normally only grownups went into space, but Samantha had been chosen from thousands of young people and was really excited.

When the plane landed Samantha and her mother came down the steps to be greeted by a band playing and lots of soldiers in uniform.

"Welcome to America," said one of the soldiers, "my name is Captain Clarke and I'm going to be looking after you during your stay."

Captain Clarke, Samantha and Angella her mum were soon being driven to the air base in an enormous car.

"This is great," said Samantha, "let's put the television on."

They played with all the gadgets in the back of the car and Samantha's mother even phoned home to say they had arrived safely.

When they arrived at the air base Captain Clarke said to Angella, "the driver will take you to your hotel, but Samantha will stay with me, she's lots to learn before she can go into space."

The rest of the day was taken up trying on space suits which you had to wear to be able to breath in space, practicing space walks and all sorts of interesting things about how to survive in space.

It was very late that night when Samantha was dropped back at the hotel by Captain Clarke.

"How was your day, it's very late, you must have been very busy?" said her mum.

"Fabulous," said Samantha, "but I'm going to bed now as I'm ever so tired and Captain Clarke said tomorrow is going to be a very busy day."

All too soon it was morning and the car arrived to take Samantha and her mum to the air base where the launch of the rocket was to take place.

It took ages getting ready, but eventually Samantha and the other astronauts had their spacesuits on and were boarding the shuttle.

Samantha waved goodbye to her mother as Captain Clarke started the countdown.

"Ten, nine, eight, seven," the rockets fired up.

"Six, five, four, three," and the power was building up.

"Two, one, zero," the bolts holding the shuttle flew off and slowly it raised from the ground, gradually getting faster and faster, flames shooting from the rockets engine.

Within minutes they were far above the ocean and looking back at the earth, it became smaller and smaller and was amazingly blue.

"Wow," said Samantha, "what a sight, I never expected it to be so blue."

"Yes," said Captain Clarke, "you are very lucky to be able to see the earth from space, not many people get the chance.

The other astronauts were very busy during the flight, doing tests and manoeuvring the shuttle, Samantha enjoyed watching and helped with many of the experiments during the mission.

In space everything is weightless which makes things float around which is very funny, but the thing Samantha enjoyed most was being able to float about the cabin upside down and to do cartwheels and backflips.

One of the astronauts had to go outside the shuttle to the payload area to launch a space satellite, which was going to beam a new television service back to earth.

Everything was going smoothly, Sergeant Thomas had opened the payload doors and released the satellite when suddenly his voice came over the intercom, "I think I have a problem."

"What's wrong, Sergeant Thomas, asked Captain Clarke.

"I've launched the satellite but my foot has got caught and I can't free it, I need help."

Captain Clarke was a very experienced astronaut and replied, "don't worry, we can find a solution to this problem, I'll check the screens to see what's wrong."

They had television cameras on the shuttle so they could see outside and soon Captain Clarke could see the problem, Sergeant Thomas had his foot stuck under a pipe right in the corner of the payload area.

"Right," said Captain Clarke, "someone will have to go outside and help free his foot, but it will have to be someone small as it's right in the corner where there is very little room." "It will have to be Samantha as she's the only one small enough to squeeze into the corner and help Sergeant Thomas."

"Be very careful when you're outside," said Captain Clarke, "don't let go for a second or you will float off into space."

Samantha put on her space helmet, "right, I'm ready," she said and was soon in the air lock and outside the space craft.

Being weightless inside was great fun, however outside was much more dangerous but she kept calm and worked her way round to where Sergeant Thomas was stuck.

It didn't take her long to see the problem and holding on with one hand she squeezed herself into the corner and freed his foot.

They both carefully worked their way back to the airlock and were soon back in the safety of the space shuttle where everyone cheered and said, "you are a very brave girl."

"Fasten seat belts," said Captain Clarke, "we're going home."

The rockets fired up and the shuttle headed towards the earth.

The journey was faultless, much to everyone's relief and they were soon landing at Kennedy Air Base.

There were enormous cheering crowds waiting to meet them, everyone was so glad to see them back, especially Samantha's mother, who rushed through the crowds and gave her a big hug, "I'm so glad to see you," she cried.

Then a tall man cane forward and shook Samantha by the hand, "I'm the President of the United States of America, we owe you so much, you're a very brave girl and a hero."

The President then placed a medal on Samantha's chest and the band started to play and everyone clapped and cheered as she stood proudly next to her mother.

Soon they were on a plane flying home, there would be many more parades when they arrived and Samantha and her mother even went on television to talk about her mission in space.

Even though Samantha was very busy, her mother still made sure she did her homework from school, which she said was very important.

The holidays rushed by and soon it was time for Samantha to go back to school, "it was hard work being a hero," said Samantha, "it will be nice to get back to school to have a rest."

31441204R00020

Printed in Great Britain
by Amazon